COVENTRY LIBRARIES

Please return this book on or before
the last date stamped below.

To renew this book take it to any of
the City Libraries before
the date due for return

Coventry City Council

Raintree is an imprint of Capstone Global Library Limited, a company incorporated in
England and Wales having its registered office at 7 Pilgrim Street, London, EC4V 6LB –
Registered company number: 6695582

www.raintree.co.uk
myorders@raintree.co.uk

Printed and bound in China.

ISBN 978-1-4062-9411-8
18 17 16 15 14
10 9 8 7 6 5 4 3 2 1

British Library Cataloguing in Publication Data
A full catalogue record for this book is available from the British Library.

Every effort has been made to contact copyright holders of material reproduced in
this book. Any omissions will be rectified in subsequent printings if notice is given to
the publisher.

All the internet addresses (URLs) given in this book were valid at the time of going to
press. However, due to the dynamic nature of the internet, some addresses may have
changed, or sites may have changed or ceased to exist since publication. While the author
and publisher regret any inconvenience this may cause readers, no responsibility for any
such changes can be accepted by either the author or the publisher.

Cover art and illustrations by Lisa K. Weber
Design: K. Carlson
Editorial: A. Deering
Production: G. Bentdahl

Acknowledgements: Shutterstock (vector images, backgrounds, paper textures)

The Case of the
HAUNTED HISTORY
MUSEUM

by Steve Brezenoff
Illustrated by Lisa K. Weber

PtERo TERROR!

LOOK UP IF YOU DARE!

MUSEUM OF NATURAL HISTORY

Pterodactyl...
Histor... um?

Pterodactylus...
from over 30...
mens, and...
those...

...not
...small,
...resent in
...e jaws, with
...nd lower hook
...than the teeth that
...ded them.

The back of the crest extended upward into a backward-
curving cone-shaped structure. The crest was com-
posed mainly of long, hard-
ened fibres (twisted together
in a spiral pattern inside the
conical part of the crest), and
covered in scales. In at least

...hat-
...about
...5 inches)
...aunt speci-
...sented by an
...ll). Other spe-
...er. However, these
...specimens have
...shown to represent ju-
...eniles of Pterodactylus, as
well as its contemporary
relatives Ctenochasma and
Germanodactylus and Gna-
thosaurus.

The skulls of adult Pterodactylus were long and
narrow with about 90 large,
conical teeth. The teeth extended back from the tips of
both jaws, and became
smaller farther away from
the jaw tips (unlike some
relatives, where teeth were
absent in the upper jaw tip
and were relatively uniform
in size). The teeth extended
farther back into the jaw
than in close relatives, as
some were present below
the front of the nasoantor-
...a fenestra, the largest

Pterodactylus, like related
pterosaurs, had a crest on its
skull composed mainly of
soft tissues. In adult Pterodactylus, this crest extended
between the back edge of the
antorbital fenestra (the largest opening in the skull) and
the back of the skull.

The neck was long, and
covered in long, bristle-like

one specimen, the crest had
a short bony base, also se
n related pterosaurs like
Germanodactylus. Solid
crests have only been found
on large, fully adult speci
mens of Pterodactylus, i
dicating that this was a di
play structure that beca
larger and more well dev
oped as

Amal Farah

Raining Sam

Wilson Kipper

Clementine Wim

Capitol City Sleuths

Amal Farah
Age: 11
Favourite Museum: Air and Space Museum
Interests: astronomy, space travel and
building models of spaceships

Raining Sam
Age: 12
Favourite Museum: History Museum
Interests: Ojibwe history, culture and
traditions, American history – good and bad

Clementine Wim
Age: 13
Favourite Museum: Museum of Art
Interests: painting, sculpting with clay and
anything colourful

Wilson Kipper
Age: 10
Favourite Museum: Natural History Museum
Interests: dinosaurs (especially pterosaurs
and herbivores) and building dinosaur models

TABLE OF

CONTENTS

CHAPTER 1
New exhibit

Wilson Kipper sat on the big stone bench in front of the Capitol City Museum of Natural History. He held his small tablet computer on his lap, studying a map of the museum as he waited for his friends to arrive.

"You're sure you're okay waiting here for your friends?" his mum, Dr Carolyn Kipper, asked. "I can stay for a few more minutes if you like."

Wilson glanced at the time in the corner of the tablet's screen. It was 9.59 a.m. "It's okay," he said. "They'll be here any minute now."

Wilson's three best friends – Amal Farah, Clementine Wim and Raining Sam – all had parents who worked at one of the museums in the Capitol City network. As they were given free passes to all of the museums, thanks to their parents' positions, the four friends took any chance they could to explore the museums together.

Today they were visiting the Natural History Museum. That meant Wilson would be the host, because his mum worked there as a paleontologist. And speaking of which...

"Mum, you'd better go inside," said

Wilson. "You're going to be late. I'll be fine." He slid his finger across the screen of his tablet and brought up the museum's website.

"Okay, okay," Dr Kipper said. "I'll leave you alone."

At that exact moment, three cyclists pulled off the nearby bike trail, heading in the direction of the museum.

"There they are," Wilson said as he clicked off his tablet and stood up to wave at his approaching friends. "Bye, Mum."

Dr Kipper waved too. Then she quickly headed into the museum to start her day at work.

Amal's sleek bike screeched to a stop in front of Wilson. Clementine, riding her old three-speed bike, and Raining, on his laid-back beach cruiser, followed behind at a much slower pace.

"Hey, Wilson," Amal said. She pushed her bike to the rack and locked it up securely.

"Hi," said Wilson. "You guys came just in time. My mum was starting to worry about leaving me out here on my own."

"Is the museum even open yet?" Raining asked as he and Clementine rolled up. Wilson was the only one of his friends who wore a watch.

"It should be opening right now," Wilson said. "Let's go inside. It's the first day of the new exhibit, and I don't want to waste a second."

"What is the exhibit about?" said

Clementine. She pulled off her cycle helmet and wiped her brow with the back of her hand.

Wilson grinned. He'd been excited about this exhibit for months – ever since his mum first told him about it. "Pterosaurs," he said.

"Ooh," said Amal. "I know about them. Flying dinosaurs, right?"

"Not exactly," Wilson said as the four friends headed up the steps to the museum. "Pterosaurs weren't dinosaurs. They were flying reptiles that lived during the age of dinosaurs. Just like ichthyosaurs weren't actually dinosaurs – they were swimming reptiles."

"Icthyo-whats?" Clementine said, furrowing her brow and looking confused.

Wilson just smiled and shook his head. He loved his friends, but Clementine's mind was usually in a bucket of paint somewhere, or sitting in a kiln with her pottery. She didn't know – or care – much about prehistoric beasts.

"Ichthyosaur," Amal said. "It means fish lizard. Doesn't it, Wilson?"

Wilson nodded. "Yep," he said as he pushed open the museum's heavy front doors.

The four friends stepped into the huge entrance hall. The Natural History Museum was the oldest museum in the Capitol City network, and you could tell the moment you walked in. Everything was wooden and heavy and looked like it had been around for decades.

Right in the entrance hall, which was so big that the Kippers' whole house could probably fit inside it, stood the most famous dinosaur skeleton in the museum's collection – the monstrous allosaurus. It was positioned so that its huge head stuck way out over the velvet rope that surrounded the skeleton. The dinosaur's huge mouth was open as if it was about to roar – or eat you.

"Whoa," said Raining, sounding impressed.

Wilson chuckled. "Oh, come on, Raining," he said. "You've seen the allosaurus model before." He used the word "model" instead of "skeleton" because it was a copy of a skeleton, not a real fossilized skeleton.

Raining shook his head, his mouth hanging open, and pointed up – way up to the high ceiling of the big entrance hall. Wilson looked up too to see what made his friend so impressed.

"Whoa," Wilson echoed when he realized what Raining was pointing at. Hanging there, with its huge wings spread wide and its long neck hanging down, was the new pterosaur model. Its enormous beak was open wide as if it would *kaw* like a giant bird.

"Did you know that the pterosaur is the largest flying animal of all time?" Wilson told his friends. He stared up at the model hanging from chains from the ceiling. "It had a wingspan of up to fourteen metres."

"Wow," said Clementine. "That's pretty amazing."

Wilson nodded. "Its name is pretty amazing too," he said. "Quetzalcoatlus. I read that it was named after the god Quetzalcoatl. The Aztecs in Central America used to worship him. His name meant 'feathered serpent'."

"I can see why," said Clementine. She stepped around the big allosaurus podium, gazing up at the quetzalcoatlus as she went. "It must have looked like a terrible dragon!"

Wilson thought it was probably much more amazing than some silly dragon from a story, but he didn't say so. Clementine was just like that – always coming up with creative stories.

"Perhaps that's where the stories came from," said Amal, walking next to Clementine.

"Don't be silly," said Wilson. "There were no people around when this creature was flying around."

"I mean perhaps people found the bones and things!" said Amal. "Just because I love space doesn't mean I have my head in the stars all the time!"

The others laughed. Amal was absolutely obsessed with astronomy, which worked out well because her father was the head archivist at the Air and Space Museum.

The four friends walked the whole length of the huge flying creature as the museum began to get crowded. It seemed as though a lot of people were excited to see the pterosaur exhibit on its first day.

"Where should we go first?" Clementine asked.

Wilson opened his mouth to say, "To the pterosaur exhibit, of course," but before he could get a word out, there was a loud *snap* from above him.

Someone shouted, "It's falling!"

Wilson looked up – as did everyone else in the museum's entrance hall – as the largest flying animal to ever exist broke free from its chains and came plummeting towards them.

CHAPTER 2
Haunted

"Look out!" Amal shouted. She threw her arms around Wilson and knocked him out of the way.

Clementine grabbed Raining by the wrist and pulled him towards the wall. All four friends dropped onto their bellies. Around them, other visitors screamed and ran.

The quetzalcoatlus crashed to the ground, smashing the allosaurus to pieces. Bits of model bone flew in every direction. All the visitors ducked and covered their faces. Little children cried and held on tight to their grown-ups.

Wilson could feel Amal's arms around him, and he didn't budge until all the noise and shouting was over. It seemed as though it went on forever.

A booming voice suddenly cut through the quiet, "Is everyone okay?" It was Lev, the museum's head of security. "Is anyone hurt?"

Amal stood up, and Wilson got to his feet as well. He took a deep, relieved breath. His friends were all right by him and okay. All the museum visitors were standing in a wide circle around the wreckage. Everyone studied the rubble nervously.

"It looks like everyone is okay," Clemetine said.

"If a little shaken up," said Lev. He put a hand on Wilson's shoulder. "You all right, Wilson?"

Wilson nodded. Then he stepped past Lev towards the middle of the hall.

"Don't get too close, please," said Lev. "We don't know if it's safe yet. I don't want anyone getting hurt – especially one of you kids."

"I know," said Wilson. "I'll be careful."

Lev stayed right behind Wilson and put a hand on his shoulder. Wilson crouched down to inspect the wreckage, while his three friends gathered around the burly security man.

"They're both ruined," Wilson said sadly.

Lev pulled off his hat and scratched his head, clicking his tongue. "This is really getting out of hand," he said.

Wilson stood and looked up at Lev. "What do you mean?" he asked. "What's getting out of hand?"

"You mean you haven't heard?" Lev said. He leaned down to speak quietly to the children, but a few other museum visitors, clearly curious about how the disaster had happened, moved closer to eavesdrop. "It's the ghosts."

Wilson squinted up at the security guard. "Ghosts?" he repeated. "Are you serious?"

Lev nodded. "I can't believe your mum hasn't mentioned it to you yet," he whispered. He looked around at the other children. "None of you have heard about this?"

Raining, Amal and Clementine all shook their heads.

"Well," Lev whispered, "I don't want this to get around too much, especially to the visitors, but – "

"Oh, I think it's too late for that," a woman behind him interrupted. She had two small children with her in a double buggy. "That's exactly why I came here this morning."

"Huh?" said Lev.

A few other visitors standing near by nodded eagerly. "We all heard about the haunting," said a man visiting with a large group of adults. "We came to see for ourselves."

Lev stood up straight and put his fists on his hips. "I suppose word's gotten out," he said, shaking his head ruefully.

"Why don't you let us in on it?" said Amal.

"Yeah," said Clementine. "I love ghost stories."

Wilson rolled his eyes. Clementine was always falling for crazy stuff like ghosts and superstitions and mind readers. To Wilson, it was all just silly stories covering up the scientific truth. Still, he wanted to hear what had been happening at the museum – and why everyone seemed to be so convinced that the place was haunted.

"It all started last week," Lev told them. "I think it was Wednesday. First the model velociraptor walked to the museum café."

"You saw it walking?!" said Amal, eyes wide.

Lev shook his head. "No," he said. "No one actually *saw* it walking. But it was in its usual spot on Tuesday night. When I unlocked the café on Wednesday morning, it was there, standing in the queue for the till."

Then it probably didn't walk there on its own, Wilson thought.

"What else?" Clementine asked, leaning closer.

"When I was locking up on Wednesday night, the lights on the second floor, the ones across the courtyard from here, flickered on and off for a few minutes," Lev said. "It certainly gave me a fright."

The security guard gestured towards the huge windows that looked out on the courtyard. Past the models of mammoths and saber-tooth cats and giant sloths, Wilson could see the office, laboratory and archives area of the museum. Most visitors never went to those areas of course, but Wilson had seen it all – his mum had showed him on his first visit.

"Anyone could have done that," Amal said, crossing her arms.

Wilson was glad she was sceptical of Lev's ghost talk. *At least I'm not the only one*, he thought.

"I thought that, too, but there's no one else in the museum at that time of night," Lev said. "It's just me and my security staff."

"Hmm…" said Amal.

Wilson still wasn't convinced. "Anything else?" he asked. "So far, all this stuff can be pretty easily explained."

"Maybe," said Lev. "But I haven't finished. On Friday morning Nancy, from the cleaning staff, and I were the first people here. The sun was hardly up. I unlocked the door, and we both saw it."

"Saw what?" Clementine asked

breathlessly. She leaned forwards, clearly excited about a good ghost sighting.

Lev's eyes went wide. "A huge, shadowy figure," he said. "It looked like it had wings as big as an aeroplane! And it was floating straight towards us, right in this very room!"

"Um," said Wilson, "wasn't that the quetzalcoatlus? The one that just came crashing down?"

Lev shook his head. "That wasn't installed until Sunday afternoon," he said. "They put it up when the pterosaur exhibit was being set up."

"I bet it's the angry spirit of a long-dead pterodactyl," said Clementine, her eyes wide and her voice pitched with excitement. "She's probably back to haunt the museum because they stole the bones of her children!"

Wilson resisted the urge to laugh at Clementine's crazy suggestion. "You actually *saw* a huge flying animal?" he asked Lev.

"Well … no," Lev admitted. "We saw its shadow, though." He pointed at the curved wall over the entrance to the ichthyosaur wing, where a giant banner now hung announcing the new pterosaur exhibit. "Right there. It took up the whole wall, so it must have come from something pretty huge."

"Or it was a huge ghost," Clementine said. "Ghosts could look like shadows, I bet."

Lev nodded eagerly.

Wilson was glad when the silly ghost talk was interrupted by a stern shout: "Everyone back away from the area, please!"

Mr Collini, the museum's director, stomped into the room. He shoved past curious bystanders and came to a stop in front of Lev. "How did this happen?" he demanded.

"All the cables snapped," Lev said, shaking his head. "Practically at the same time."

"Hmm," said Mr Collini. He stepped carefully into the rubble and found one of the cables that had been holding up the quetzalcoatlus. "How could that have happened?"

Mr Collini pulled the length of cable until he found its end. Wilson caught a glimpse. The end looked too neat to have snapped.

"Isn't it obvious?" said Lev. "It's the ghosts."

Mr Collini sighed. He dug the velvet rope and metal posts, some of which had fallen over, from beneath the mess of model bones. Lev helped him set the barrier back up around the wreckage.

While they worked, Wilson took the opportunity to whisper to his friends. "Did you see the end of the cable? It was clean, not frayed."

"As if someone had cut it?" Clementine asked.

Wilson nodded. "Exactly."

"So either there's a ghost in the museum with a pair of cable cutters in its pocket," said Amal, "or this wasn't the work of any ghost at all."

CHAPTER 3
On the case

Later that day, after the mess in the museum's entrance hall had finally been contained, Wilson, Clementine, Raining and Amal sat on the ragged old sofa in Dr Kipper's office.

The museum had been closed to the public for the rest of the day as a result of the accident, but the four friends were allowed to stay – as long as they kept out of the way.

"I just can't imagine what's come over everyone here," Dr Kipper said, pacing back and forth in front of them. "Practically every member of the museum's staff, including a handful of actual scientists, is *convinced* we're dealing with ghosts."

"It's crazy," Wilson agreed, shaking his head.

"Madness," Amal said.

"So weird," said Raining.

"Well, I like it," said Clementine, sounding energized. "It's exciting. Thanks for letting us use your office, Dr Kipper."

"You're very welcome, Clementine," Dr Kipper said. "As long as the museum is closed to visitors, you're welcome to stay here."

Just then, the phone on Dr Kipper's desk started ringing loudly, and she quickly grabbed it. "Paleontology, this is Dr Kipper speaking," she said. "Mmhm … wait, what? Are you joking?" She sighed heavily. "Fine. I'll be there in five minutes."

Wilson's mother hung up and sighed again. "This is getting ridiculous," she said, running her hand over her close-cut curly hair. "Mr Collini has called in the experts."

"You mean a detective?" Raining asked.

"The police?" Amal said.

"The MythBusters?" Wilson guessed, crossing his arms.

Dr Kipper shook her head. "Worse," she said. "Ghost hunters – including a psychic."

At that, Clementine sat straight up. "Ooh," she said. "Can we watch them ghost hunt?"

"I don't think so," said Dr Kipper firmly. "You kids need to stay in here. I, on the other hand, have to go and meet with the psychic."

"What?" said Wilson. "Why?"

"All the staff have to do it," his mum told him. "I assume it's Mr Collini's orders."

"But what about us?" said Wilson. "Do we have to just sit here?"

Dr Kipper grabbed her blazer from the back of her desk chair and slipped it on. "I'd stay out of sight if I were you," she said. "If the ghost hunters see you, they'll either make you talk to their psychic or they'll think you're a ghost."

"Or zap us or something," Raining muttered.

Dr Kipper laughed. "I don't think we have to worry about that, but it's better for you to stay here. Just in case." With that, she left the office, closing the door behind her.

"Well," said Amal, standing up, "we're obviously not staying here when there's a mystery to solve."

The others stood up too. "Or a ghost to find!" said Clementine, looking excited by the possibility.

"As long as we don't get zapped," said Raining.

"Or caught," Wilson said. "I don't think my mum would be very happy about that."

The four friends slipped quickly and quietly out of Dr Kipper's office. With the place officially closed, the museum halls were eerily silent, and most of the lights had been switched off. Only a few emergency lights and the glowing red exit signs lit their way as they crept back into the exhibit.

"I bet the ghost hunters told them to leave all the lights off," Clementine whispered. "I've read that that's the only way ghosts will come out. They don't like electricity."

"Or they just want to keep everyone afraid," said Wilson, "so they can charge the museum as much as they want for their services."

"Leave me alone," Clementine said. "I'll believe what I want."

"Where should we start?" Amal asked, trying to get them to focus. "We all saw the big pterosaur fall. Should we start in the entrance hall? Or go and investigate one of the locations Lev mentioned for the other three 'haunting' incidents?"

"The entrance is probably crawling with maintenance staff by now," Wilson pointed out. "And besides, we already know those cables were cut. I say we start with the velociraptor."

"It won't be in the museum café anymore," said Raining.

"Then we're off to the theropod hall," said Wilson. "This way."

The four sleuths crept up the wide, central staircase towards the museum's first floor.

"Isn't the café in the basement?" said Clementine.

Wilson nodded. "Yeah, why?"

Clementine looked thoughtful. "I was just thinking that if someone moved the velociraptor, they would've had to carry it down all these steps," she said. "Pretty hard work."

"Or they could have used the goods lift," Wilson said. "It's at the back of the building near the offices."

"Hmm," said Clementine. "I suppose that's possible…"

The upper level of the museum was even quieter than the main floor had been.

"I suppose the ghost hunters haven't finished exploring downstairs yet," Amal said. She led the way through the wide hallway, past darkened archways and dinosaur posters.

At the far end of the main corridor, two troodon models, replete with feathers, flanked a slender, tall archway. They looked like ornately coloured birds and were as tall as Clementine – and almost as brightly coloured as her paint-splattered t-shirt and jeans.

"There it is," said Wilson, picking up the pace and moving past Amal to lead the group. "The theropod hall."

The four sleuths stepped through the archway into the eerily lit exhibit. In the dim light, the theropod models cast long, flickering shadows across the enormous room.

"So, Wilson," said Amal. Her voice shook a little, but she tried hard not to sound scared. "What is a theropod, anyway? Aren't these just plain old dinosaurs?"

"It's a bit confusing," Wilson whispered as they prowled slowly through the display hall. "Theropods mainly walked on two legs, but they often had some feathers. And then later on, they evolved into birds. In fact, birds are theropods."

"Whoa," said Raining. "You mean the sparrows living in our garden are dinosaurs?"

"Well, dinosaur cousins, anyway," Wilson said with a shrug. "But they are technically theropods."

Just then Wilson spotted the model of the velociraptor skeleton. It stood near the emergency exit. Under the glowing red exit sign, the creature looked even more scary. "There it is," he said.

The four friends stood around the fearsome-looking model. It looked like an enormous sprinting bird with its long neck and head lurched forwards. The

velociraptor's long tail pointed straight back behind it, helping to balance the creature as it ran. The dinosaur's arms were bent and close to its sides, the way a bird pulls in its wings, and its mouth was wide open, showing a maw full of sharp, curved teeth.

"Blimey, that's scary," Raining said, shuddering slightly. "I definitely would *not* want to see that thing chasing after me. So what do we do now? Dust for fingerprints or something?"

"I don't know if fingerprints will help," Wilson said. "Even if we knew how to get a good print off a model, we don't exactly have the police database of fingerprints to compare them to."

Clementine got as close to the model

as the velvet rope allowed. "Did this thing have feathers too?" she asked.

"Yup," said Wilson.

Amal leaned back against the emergency exit door and yawned. "This is a waste of time," she said. "There's nothing here."

Suddenly, she yelped as the emergency door behind her opened and she fell back into an unlit cement corridor. "Ow!" Before she'd even hit the hard, cold floor of the corridor, red lights flashed and a screeching siren wailed.

"Are you okay?" Clementine shouted, running to Amal's side. She helped her to her feet, then pulled her back into the theropod hall. Together the two girls swung the heavy emergency door closed tight. But even with the door closed, the alarm kept screaming, and the lights kept flashing.

"Oh, no," Wilson said. "We're going to be in big trouble."

Just then, they heard loud, hurried footsteps – lots of them – coming from the first-floor's main hall. "It's coming from in there!" shouted an excited voice. "Bring the equipment!"

Torch beams suddenly swung into the room, nearly illuminating the four friends still gathered around the shrieking emergency exit.

"It's the ghost hunters!" Clementine whispered. She probably wanted to run over and join them.

"We have to get out of here," Wilson

said. He looked around, but the only exit, other than the main archway, was the emergency door Amal had just stumbled upon.

Wilson took a deep breath and slammed the door open again. "Come on," he said. "Run!"

Beyond the door was a long, cold, cement corridor. Small lights positioned close to the floor provided the only light source.

"Where are we?" Raining asked, looking a little concerned.

"I don't know," Wilson admitted. "I've never been here before." He glanced around for a clue as to where they were, but the corridor stretched off in both directions with no markings except for a few glowing exit signs. "Let's try this way."

Wilson led them to the right, around a corner and past several unmarked black doors. The dimly lit corridor finally ended at a pair of heavy-looking, bashed-up red doors.

"Goods lift," Wilson said. He pressed the down button. "We can get back to my mum's office from here. I know where this stops on the ground floor."

Wilson poked the button again and again, wishing it would hurry up. A moment later, the doors slid open, and the four of them stepped inside.

Amal reached out to push the button for the ground floor, but Wilson grabbed her wrist to stop her. "Wait a minute," he said. "I have an idea." Instead, he pushed the button marked "B" – for basement.

CHAPTER 4
Busted!

After a loud, slow ride, the lift clunked to a stop on the lowest level of the museum. Wilson stepped slowly off, squinting into the unfamiliar darkness. This basement was nearly pitch black.

"Where are we?" Raining whispered, stepping off the lift behind him. "Other than the basement, I mean."

"I don't know," said Wilson. "Put your hand on my shoulder so we don't get separated."

Raining did. It helped to know his friend was right there with him. "Clementine, Amal," Wilson said. "Form a chain."

Together, the four friends moved slowly into the darkness. Wilson's eyes were gradually becoming accustomed to the lack of light, and soon he saw little spots scattered all over, as if tiny specks were reflecting off hundreds of things in the room.

Suddenly Wilson bumped into something hard and cold, and there was a loud clatter of metal as whatever he'd hit crashed to the ground.

"Shh!" said Amal.

"Sorry!" said Wilson. "I walked into something."

"I guessed that," Amal said wryly.

"There's good news, though," Wilson said. "I know where we are now, and at least part of the mystery is solved."

"Care to let the rest of us in on it?" Clementine said from the back of the group.

Wilson didn't have to say a word, though. A moment later he pushed open a swinging door, and they stepped into a room flooded with green-tinted sunlight coming through the window wells in the courtyard.

"The museum café," Wilson said. "The

goods lift must open into it. So now we know how the velociraptor got down here."

Clementine nodded. "Yep," she said, putting her hands on her hips. "It took the goods lift. Clever dinosaur."

Wilson rolled his eyes. "You mean someone put it on a trolly and wheeled it onto the lift," he said.

"Or that," Clementine admitted with a shrug.

"Okay," said Amal, stepping between Clementine and Wilson, "so someone brought the dinosaur down here on the goods lift. But who?"

"Who would want to?" asked Raining.

"You know what they always say about solving a mystery," Amal said, hopping up on the edge of a café table. "Follow the money."

Raining, Clementine and Wilson all took seats at the table around Amal.

"I don't understand how fake ghost sightings would make anyone any money, though," Clementine said.

The friends sat in silence for a few moments, thinking, but no one else seemed to have any ideas either.

"I suppose we'd better get back to my mum's office," Wilson finally said, standing up. "She might be finished with her meeting with the psychics by now. And I don't want her to get back and realize we're not there."

The others sighed and got to their feet as well. They all went through the main café doors, but they'd barely taken a few steps when they heard excited whispers from around the corner.

"Shh," Wilson said. He quickly ushered his friends back into the café, and they stood by the door to listen. A moment later, they heard a girl's voice, followed by the laughter of more girls.

"It's Ruthie Rothchild!" Clementine said. "I'd recognize that voice anywhere."

Amal clapped her hand over Clementine's mouth to silence her. "Keep it down. Let's see what she's up to."

"There won't be anyone in there," Ruthie was saying as the small group of girls approached. "We can take as much ice cream from the freezer as we can carry!"

"Yeah," said another voice – Ruthie's friend Sloan. "Then we can sell them to the people waiting outside."

The four sleuths hurried away from the café door as the girls' voices drew closer. "Back in the kitchen," Wilson hissed. "Quick."

The others followed him, and they pushed through the swinging doors to the kitchen, then huddled together behind a metal cabinet where they wouldn't be seen. "Once they grab the goodies," Wilson said, "we'll jump out. Catch them red-handed."

Clementine nodded and smiled. Wilson knew how pleased she would be to get Ruthie in big trouble for something like this. And if Ruthie had anything to do with the haunting, it would make Clementine's day.

The two girls had known each other since they were young, and they didn't exactly get along.

Amal peeked carefully around the cabinet and watched as Ruthie and her gang pushed open the swinging doors and headed straight towards the big industrial freezer.

"They're going in there now," Amal said. "It's Sloan and Ruthie and that new girl from school. Sierra, I think her name is Sierra."

"She certainly made friends with the wrong group," Clementine said, shaking her head.

"Okay," said Amal. "They're opening the freezer. Ruthie has a big bag to carry the ice cream."

"So it's premeditated," Wilson said. "She planned this."

"They're filling it up," Amal said.

"That must be fifty ice cream bars and lollies and cones!" Clementine said. "Oh, they are in so much trouble." She leapt out from their hiding place, and the four of them sprinted over to the ice-cream-thieving girls before they even knew what was happening.

"Busted!" Clementine said, snatching the bag out of Ruthie's hand.

Ruthie rolled her eyes. "Fine," she said. "You caught us. Put the ice cream back and we'll leave."

"Oh, no," said Amal, stepping right up to Ruthie. "You're not walking away from this. We're going to tell Lev."

"Oh, please," said Sloan. "That nitwit is so caught up with this haunting stuff, he won't care about some stupid ice cream. Besides, we'll deny it. It'll be your word against ours. Why would he believe you?"

"Maybe because my mum works here," Wilson said.

"Exactly," Clementine said, looking pleased. "Like I said, busted."

Ruthie didn't respond. She didn't even look at Clementine. "Come on, you two," she said to her friends. "Let's go. It's not like they can arrest us." She and Sloan strutted across the café. But the new girl, Sierra, hesitated.

"Do you want to say something?" Amal asked.

The new girl opened her mouth to speak, but Ruthie called from the doorway, "Come on, Sierra. You don't have to talk to them."

"If you lot had anything to do with the weird stuff going on here," Wilson said quickly, "you can tell us. We know it was all Ruthie's idea."

"Sierra!" Ruthie snapped.

If the new girl had wanted to say something, she didn't anymore. She hurried after Ruthie and Sloan as they left the café.

"What was that about?" Amal said.

"I don't know. It seemed as if she wanted to tell us something," Wilson said.

"Maybe she's not as awful as Ruthie

and Sloan," Clementine said, taking a step towards the café doors. "Maybe she feels bad for getting mixed up with those two criminals."

"And maybe they *are* involved in what's been going on here," Amal said, pressing her hands together. "Maybe she wanted to confess. Maybe she wanted to tell us everything!"

Wilson bit his lip. It didn't seem quite right. How would Ruthie and her friends have moved the velociraptor and made the quetzalcoatlus fall?

"Let's get back to my mum's office," he said. "She'll be there soon."

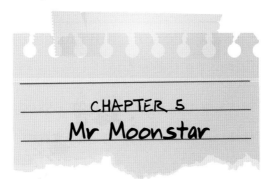

CHAPTER 5
Mr Moonstar

Dr Kipper's office was empty when they got there, but not for long. The four of them had hardly taken their seats when Dr Kipper swept into the room – and she wasn't alone.

Before anyone could say anything, a man wearing a long, silvery robe and an array of colourful beaded necklaces trailed into the office after her. Mr Collini followed closely behind. "Here they are, Mr Moonstar," he said, waving towards the children on the sofa.

"What's going on?" Wilson asked, looking back and forth between the grown-ups.

"Kids," said Mr Collini, "this is Mr Moonstar. He's the psychic who's been investigating what's been happening here at the museum. As you were all right there when the quetzalcoatlus fell, I thought it might be helpful if he spoke with you. You can tell him about your spiritual experience at the time of the incident."

"'Spiritual experience'?" Amal repeated, raising an eyebrow.

"Do we have to?" Wilson asked, looking at his mother.

Dr Kipper sighed, but she nodded gently. "Let's just consider it a favour to the museum," she said with a smile.

Wilson knew what his mum really meant. She thought it was silly – and probably a waste of time – but it was what Mr Collini wanted. And with the museum director's reputation for having a bad temper, it was best to do what he wanted.

"Ugh!" Amal grumbled, slouching back on the sofa. "This is so silly."

Wilson leaned close to his friend. "Remember what happened to Dr Lin," he said. "Let's just get it over with."

Dr Lin, the museum's former head of paleontology, had been fired only a few weeks before. Wilson and his friends had all been in the prehistoric mammals exhibit when it happened. It seemed that Dr Lin hadn't agreed with Mr Collini's ideas about how to dress the early humans in a display of mammoths. Dr Lin had wanted it to be accurate; Mr Collini had wanted it to be exciting. It was that difference of opinion that had led to Dr Lin's departure.

Thankfully, the interview didn't take long. Mr Moonstar asked about any chills they might have felt before the model fell. Then he asked if any of them had been visited by ghosts lately, or ever. Only Clementine had a story for that question. Mr Moonstar was *very* interested, even though it had happened five years earlier when Clementine and her mother had visited some old churches in Venice during a family trip to Italy.

"Do you think it might have something to do with this?" Clementine said, leaning forwards on the sofa eagerly.

"All things are connected," Mr Moonstar said, clasping his hands together in front of his face, "in the spirit world."

"Whoa…" said Clementine. She was easily impressed by such talk.

When he was finished, Mr Moonstar bowed to them and left. Mr Collini hurried down the corridor after the psychic, peppering him with questions about the children and whether any of them might be responsible for the haunting.

Dr Kipper looked exhausted as she checked the time. "They're opening the café so staff and anyone else stuck inside the museum during this fiasco can have lunch," she said. "Why don't you four go and get something to eat?"

CHAPTER 6
Any suspects?

As the four friends walked to the museum café, they discussed the case and what they knew so far.

"Do we have any suspects?" Amal asked.

"Apart from the spirit of a long-dead pterodactyl mother?" Clementine said with a laugh. "How about Ruthie and company?"

Wilson wasn't so sure. "Remember what Amal said," he reminded his friends. "It's the key to most mysteries: follow the money."

"So who makes money from the museum closing?" Raining said. "Certainly not Mr Collini."

"That's a good point," said Wilson. In his mind, he crossed Mr Collini off the suspect list.

"But, Wilson," Clementine interjected, "Ruthie was going to make money! Don't you remember? She and her friends were going to sell the ice cream they stole from the café to the people waiting outside to get back in."

"That's true," Amal agreed thoughtfully.

Clementine grinned. Wilson could tell she was hoping this would be the perfect chance to bust Ruthie for something big.

"We should look into it," Wilson conceded. "But I don't know if she had the opportunity to pull off all the tricks Lev told us about."

"Not to mention dropping that huge quetzl-what-do-you-call-it from the ceiling like that," Raining said.

The café was buzzing when they walked in. All the scientists and staff, all the ghost hunters, even Mr Collini was there, and everyone was chattering about ghosts they'd seen.

Every table was full, but Wilson spotted Ruthie, Sloan and Sierra in the far corner, sitting in a little circle. "There they are," he said.

"Let's see if we can get Sierra alone," Clementine said. "I think she wants to confess."

"I'll take care of it," Amal said. She strode right up to the three girls and said, "Sierra. The head of security wants to talk to you."

"Me?" Sierra said, looking worried. She glanced over at Ruthie for help.

Ruthie just rolled her eyes. "Well, tell him we don't want to talk to him," she snapped.

"Well, lucky for you, he just wants Sierra," Amal said. "He's waiting outside the café."

Sierra looked at Ruthie again, then at Sloan, but the other girls just shrugged. Reluctantly, Sierra got up and followed Amal out into the corridor. Clementine, Wilson and Raining all trailed close behind them.

When they left the café, Sierra glanced around the empty corridor. "Where – hey, what is this?" she said. She grabbed for the doors to go back inside, but Amal blocked her way.

"We know Ruthie's been up to no good," Clementine said. "We know it's not your fault. We don't want you to get in trouble for her."

"So why don't you tell us what she's been doing?" Amal said.

Sierra looked confused. "Huh? But you already stopped her. Don't you remember?" she said. "We were going to steal some ice cream?"

"Yeah," said Clementine slowly, "but what else? Wasn't Ruthie behind all the weird ghost stuff that's been happening?"

"What?" Sierra said. She shook her head. "No. That's ridiculous. Didn't you see all the ghost hunters and the psychic running around? This isn't some practical joke. It's the real thing."

"Oh, come on," said Amal, rolling her eyes.

"Look," Sierra said, pulling her phone from her pocket. She poked around and then held it up to show off a local news website. The entire page was covered with headlines about the museum – especially about Mr Moonstar.

"See?" Sierra said. "Everyone's saying it's real. Mr Moonstar is becoming totally famous."

"Wait, I'm confused," Raining said. "Didn't you want to tell us something before?"

"Perhaps that Ruthie has been behind all this?" Amal suggested.

"No," said Sierra, shaking her head. "I wanted to tell you she was bad news – much worse than I thought. I didn't think I wanted to be friends with her and Sloan anymore. I was hoping I could be friends with you instead."

"Oh," said Amal.

"That makes sense," said Clementine. "Do you still want to?"

Sierra shrugged one shoulder. "I don't know," she said. "You lot are being pretty weird. Besides, Ruthie's mum gave me a lift here, so I'd better go back with her." With that, she slipped back into the café.

CHAPTER 7
Ghost hunters

"Well, that was a dead end," Wilson said a few minutes later. He took a bite from his hot dog as he walked. They each had one. It was the only thing they could grab and take with them.

"Still," Clementine said, "at least she's not as horrible as Ruthie, right?"

"I suppose," Wilson said. "But she also gave us other important info – Mr Moonstar."

"What about him?" Raining asked, sounding confused.

"I get it," Amal said. "Follow the money. Moonstar's doing very well today. His team of ghost hunters are getting paid to be here, and he's probably getting the most fame he's ever seen."

"Exactly," said Wilson. "Let's see if we can track him down. I didn't see him in the café."

It took quite a while to find Mr Moonstar. The four of them wandered the wide, echoing halls as lunchtime ended and the lights went off, signifying that the ghost hunt was on again.

"Great," said Clementine sarcastically. "So the lights are off, and now the dinosaur spirits will find us."

"Hopefully the ghost hunters will," said Amal. "That's probably the fastest way to find Moonstar in this humungous place."

As it turned out, she was right. As the four sleuths turned a corner, they were nearly blinded by four super-bright torches.

"Who's there?" one of the ghost hunters shouted. They hurried down the hall and surrounded the children. They all carried torches and special goggles, plus big, heavy-looking rucksacks with antennae sticking out all over the place.

"Just a bunch of kids," said the lead ghost hunter.

"Just a bunch of ghost hunters," Amal retorted.

"Have you found any poltergeists yet?" Clementine asked.

"The investigation is still in progress," said one of the hunters. "And we only report to Mr Moonstar."

"Of course," said Wilson. "And where *is* Mr Moonstar?"

"He's still doing interviews," one of the ghost hunters said. "Check Collini's office."

"He's interviewing Collini?" Wilson asked.

"Nah," said the hunter. "Collini was his first interview. No spiritual involvement there at all. This interview is with some doctor who used to work here. I think he was in charge of the dinosaur exhibition or something. We found him skulking around in the pterosaur exhibit."

Wilson could hardly believe it. This could be a great lead. "You mean Dr Lin?" he said. "He's here?"

"That sounds right," said the hunter. "Now if you'll excuse us, we still have a lot of ground to cover."

The group of ghost hunters hurried away, and Wilson turned to his friends. "Maybe money isn't the issue after all," he said. "Maybe it's revenge."

CHAPTER 8
A new suspect

"Dr Lin?" Wilson said as the former head of paleontology finally stepped out of Mr Collini's office.

Wilson and his friends had been waiting just outside the closed door for almost half an hour hoping to bump into the doctor.

Dr Lin's interview with Mr Moonstar must have been a lot tougher than ours, Wilson thought.

"Wilson Kipper!" Dr Lin said with a big smile. He certainly didn't seem to be feeling angry or vengeful – at all. "How are you? I haven't seen you in quite some time."

"Um, I'm well, thanks," said Wilson. "How about you?" He'd always liked Dr Lin. The former head paleontologist had always been great about not treating Wilson like a little child.

Dr Lin shook his head gravely. "I'm okay. I wish I could say the same for the museum. There are certainly some strange things happening down here today, eh?" he said.

"Does Mr Moonstar think you're involved?" Clementine asked. "Spiritually, I mean."

Dr Lin grinned. "He might!" he said. "I have no idea. He's a … hard man to read."

"Dr Lin," Wilson said. "I don't want to be rude, but I have to ask you. Why are you here today? Didn't Mr Collini – I mean…"

"Yes, I was fired," Dr Lin admitted sadly. "And trust me when I tell you that being back here at the museum isn't easy. It brings back a lot of memories. But Wilson, you know better than any other person – what has my number-one obsession always been?"

Wilson knew because it was the same as his. "Pterosaurs," he said.

Dr Lin nodded and smiled. "I couldn't miss the grand opening of the new exhibit," he said. "After all, your mother and I worked very hard to make it so special."

"That's true," Wilson said. He realized it had been silly to think Dr Lin would be involved with anything so harmful to the museum's exhibits. He'd always taken such great care of them when he worked there.

"I came for the opening, and when they locked the front doors I knew Lev would start questioning everyone outside," Dr Lin explained. "So instead of going outside, I hurried deeper into the museum, thinking I could find somewhere to hide until this blew over."

Wilson assumed that plan hadn't gone very well given that Dr Lin had just left a lengthy interview with the head ghost hunter.

Dr Lin shook his head. "Not my best idea," he admitted. "I should have thought it through. When Mr Moonstar's ghost hunters found me, they thought I was up to no good."

"You can't blame them. That does sort of make sense," Amal said.

Dr Lin shrugged. "I haven't done anything wrong, so I suppose we'll just have to wait and see what conclusions they come to," he said. "Anyway, it was nice to see you, Wilson." With a wave goodbye, the doctor headed off down the corridor.

"Well, at least that's one suspect eliminated. But that still leaves Moonstar," Raining said.

The four friends stepped into Collini's office and found Mr Moonstar sitting on the carpet with his eyes closed and his legs crossed.

"Do you think he's asleep?" Raining whispered.

"He's meditating," Clementine said, leaning down to look into the psychic's peaceful-looking face. "At least I think that's what he's doing."

Just then, the phone on Mr Collini's desk started ringing. It rang and rang.

More lights lit up on the phone. It seemed as though every line in the museum was ringing at the same time.

"Can't he hear that?" Amal said. She waved a hand back and forth in front of Mr Moonstar, and the psychic smiled a little, even though he never once opened his eyes.

"I hear all," Mr Moonstar said in a calm, monotone voice. "Alas, it is not my phone."

"That's true," said Wilson. "It's Mr Collini's." He stepped up to the desk, cleared his throat and picked up the still-ringing phone.

"What are you doing?" Clementine said urgently. "Let it ring!"

Wilson shook his head, hit the button for line one and said in his deepest and most serious voice, "This is Mr Collini."

After a few moments of listening quietly, Wilson hung up the phone. He grinned at his friends and said, "I think we have a new suspect."

CHAPTER 9
Cracking the case

"I don't get it," said Raining as the four friends hurried down the main steps of the museum. "Who was on the phone?"

"Journalists," Wilson said, glancing back over his shoulder at his friends. "Newspapers, radio and TV – local and national."

"And that made you decide Moonstar isn't behind this?" Amal asked. "I'm with Raining – I don't get it."

Amal and Raining sounded confused, but Clementine was nodding in understanding. "He never really made sense as a suspect," she said. "Even if he had cut the cables on the quetzalcoatlus, he certainly wasn't around last week to flicker the lights and drag a dinosaur skeleton halfway across the museum just to scare Lev."

"Exactly," said Wilson. "But one person had both the opportunity *and* the motive for all the alleged ghost acts – Mr Collini."

"Mr Collini?" Amal said. "But what was *his* motive?"

"Don't you see?" Wilson said as the four swung around the staircase and hurried to the big entrance hall. "This is great publicity for the museum."

They reached the entrance and found Dr Kipper, Mr Collini and Lev standing in the now-empty centre of the hall. The remains of the quetzlcoatlus and the allosaurus – its first victim in more than sixty million years – had been cleared away.

"Wilson," Dr Kipper said, "what are you four doing here? Did you have some lunch?"

"Yeah, we did," Wilson said. "Hey, Mr Collini, I was wondering, how did the promotion go for the new pterosaur exhibit?"

"It went well," said Mr Collini. "Why do you ask?"

"I don't remember seeing anything about it in the paper," Amal said.

"There was a small article," Dr Kipper pointed out. "I remember seeing it in *The Daily Post*."

"Ah, yes," said Mr Collini, frowning. But he brightened quickly and waved his arms towards the crowd still waiting outside in the summer heat. "But look! It worked wonders. Look at the crowd out there."

"You think they're here for the pterosaurs?" Lev asked. He shook his head. "I think it's the ghosts that are bringing them out today." He turned to the children. "That's exactly what that woman told us this morning, remember?"

"Ha!" Mr Collini laughed nervously. "That's ridiculous. If they wanted ghosts they'd wait for Halloween."

"Do you think so?" Wilson said suspiciously.

Mr Collini didn't reply. Instead, he checked his watch. "I should really be getting back to my office," he muttered, walking away.

Amal grabbed his arm to stop him. "Mr Collini," she said. "Do you have a key to all the emergency exits in the building?"

"Well, of course I do," he replied. "But why?"

"Then the alarms wouldn't go off if you used an emergency door," Wilson continued.

"And of course you have access to the gantry above us right now?" Clementine said.

"Naturally I do, but – " Mr Collini started to say.

"You must work some very long hours, too," Raining interrupted him. "You're probably here all the time. Even when there are only a couple of security guards roaming the halls, perhaps someone from the cleaning staff?"

Mr Collini opened his mouth to speak, but nothing came out.

"What are you kids getting at?" said Lev.

Wilson didn't have to answer. He could see the gears turning in Lev's mind, and a moment later, Lev turned to Mr Collini.

"Hey, wait a minute," he said. *"You're* the ghost, aren't you?"

"Mr Collini!" Dr Kipper said, looking horrified. "Is that true?"

Mr Collini didn't speak, but his cheeks turned red.

"I can't believe this!" Dr Kipper exclaimed. "You destroyed our quetzalcoatlus and allosaurus models! You could have seriously hurt someone!"

"Please understand!" Mr Collini said. "I didn't intend to hurt anyone. I didn't even mean to break anything! I only cut one cable. I thought the giant thing would soar across the lobby as if it had come back to life."

"But why?" Dr Kipper asked.

"Publicity!" Mr Collini said. "I'm no scientist, Carolyn. My job is to bring in the money. And for money, we need visitors."

Lev shook his head and pulled the set of handcuffs from his belt. "I'm sorry, Mr Collini," he said. "But this is a matter for the Capitol City police."

"I know, I know," said Mr Collini. For a moment he looked upset, but when he caught sight of the crowds milling around outside, waiting to come in, he smiled again. "But look at all the people! It worked! The museum will have its best day in years."

With that, Lev led him away, towards the security room, to wait for the police.

"See?" Amal whispered to her friends. "I told you – follow the money."

"There's still one thing I don't understand, though," Clementine said. "What about the giant flying ghost Lev saw?"

Wilson stepped behind the front desk. He had a feeling he'd find what he wanted, and he did – a big, heavy torch like the ones the security team carried. Right next to it sat a small plastic model of a pterosaur.

Wilson clicked on the torch, held up the pterosaur toy and cast its shadow on the far wall. It was huge. "Easy," he said, grinning at Clementine. "Now let's see if we can get the lights switched back on. I still want to see the pterosaur exhibit before closing time."

Steve B.

About the Author

Steve Brezenoff is the author of more than fifty middle-school chapter books, including the Field Trip Mysteries series, the Ravens Pass series of thrillers and the Return to Titanic series. In his spare time, he enjoys video games, cycling and cooking. Steve lives in Minnesota, USA, with his wife, Beth, and their son and daughter.

Lisa W.

About the Illustrator

Lisa K. Weber is an illustrator currently living in California, USA. She graduated from Parsons School of Design in 2000 and then began freelancing. Since then, she has completed many print, animation and design projects, including graphic novelizations of classic literature, character and background designs for children's cartoons and textiles for dog clothing.

GLOSSARY

confess admit something, usually something you did that was wrong

exhibition display or show that is usually open to the public

motive reason why a person did something

paleontologist scientist who studies fossils and other ancient life

poltergeist ghost that makes its presence known through noises or by moving objects around

psychic person who claims to sense supernatural forces

publicity information about a person or event meant to draw people's attention and get them interested

revenge act of getting back at someone for injuring or harming you or someone you care about

sceptical not believing that something or someone is truthful

sleuth someone who solves mysteries or is good at finding out facts

DISCUSSION QUESTIONS

1. Which dinosaur was your favourite? Talk about your reasoning.

2. Who did you think was going to be behind the strange events at the museum? Discuss why you thought that person was guilty.

2. Mr Collini thought the only good way to advertise the exhibit was to make up a story about a ghost. Can you think of any better ways to advertise? Talk about how you would let people know about the new exhibit.

WRITING PROMPTS

1. Imagine you discovered a new dinosaur. Write a paragraph about what it looks like, what it eats and what makes it special.

2. Imagine that there really was a ghost in the museum. Write a paragraph describing how the story would be different.

3. Sierra wasn't comfortable with Ruthie and the other girls stealing ice cream. Have your friends ever tried to make you do something that you didn't want to do? Write about your experience. Explain what you did and why.

NATURAL HISTORY INFORMATION

The Natural History Museum in London opened its doors to the public for the very first time in April 1881. Since then, it has become a popular visitor attraction, and one of the most visited museums in the world. It is home to more than 70 million **specimens**, ranging from **microscopic slides** to **mammoth skeletons**! The museum welcomes more than five million people each year and is dedicated to sharing knowledge by encouraging curiosity and enjoyment of the natural world.

It is possible to see:

* 55 million animals, including 28 million insects
* 9 million **fossils**
* 6 million plant specimens
* more than 500,000 rocks and minerals
* 3,200 meteorites.

DINOSAUR FACTS

Richard Owen, a British paleontologist, invented the word "dinosaur" in 1842. He combined the Greek words "deinos" (awe-inspiring) and "sauros" (lizard) to form "dinosaur."

Dinosaurs lived from 230 million to 65 million years ago in what is called the **Mesozoic Era**. The Mesozoic Era is broken into three periods: the **Triassic**, **Jurassic** and the **Cretaceous**.

Capable of growing throughout their whole life, dinosaurs could get very large. The longest dinosaur ever found is the **seismosaurus** at 30 metres long, the tallest is the **brachiosaurus** at 12 metres and the heaviest is the **argentinosaurus** at around 72 tonnes.

Dinosaurs are often put into one of two groups: herbivores and carnivores. **Herbivores** only ate plants and **carnivores** only ate meat. If a dinosaur had flat teeth, it was most likely to be a herbivore. If it had curved, pointed or serrated teeth, it was most likely to be a carnivore.